The Pony that went to Sea

First published in Great Britain 1997 by Heinemann and Mammoth,
imprints of Reed International Books Ltd
Michelin House, 81 Fulham Rd, London, SW3 6RB
and Auckland, Melbourne, Singapore and Toronto

10 9 8 7 6 5 4 3 2 1

Paperback ISBN 0 7497 3112 5
Hardback ISBN 0 434 97984 8
A CIP catalogue record for this title is available
from the British Library

Printed and bound in China

K. M. PEYTON

The Pony that went to Sea

Illustrated by **Anna C. Leplar**

 **YELLOW BANANAS**

Chapter One

WHEN THE TRAVELLERS camping by the river
departed, they left behind a small, old pony
called Paddy. Although he whinnied to his
owners as they drove away down the road,
nobody took any notice of him. They didn't
want him any more because he was old and
had bad legs. It was winter and the weather
was cold, and Paddy had only a small patch
of grazing and no shelter.

There were no houses nearby, only a
houseboat that was moored on the river.

It had once been a small inshore cargo boat. All its cargo space had been turned into living quarters by its owner, Mr Tarboy. It was very snug with a big coal stove to warm it and a proper kitchen (called a galley) and little bedrooms each for his children, Tom and Emily. On deck there was a wheel-house and a lean-to shed behind it, which Mr Tarboy had built to shelter his stock of timber and useful bits and pieces. There was a long gangplank from the deck to the bank. When the tide was high the boat rose up on the water and you could see over the fields, and when the tide went out the boat sank down and sat on the mud, but it didn't go anywhere any more.

That morning, when
the boat rose up on
the tide, Emily looked
out of her bedroom
porthole and saw that the
travellers had gone.

She rushed to tell her parents.

'Good thing too, I reckon,' her mother said.
'All those dogs barking and the rubbish
lying about.'

'They did no harm,' said Mr Tarboy.
'They never bothered us.'

'They liked us,' Tom said.

When he walked to school with Emily, the
travellers had always smiled and shouted
hello and the dogs were friendly. He was
rather sad they had gone. It was quite lonely
living on the river. Their friends all lived in
the village a mile up the road.

Tom and Emily got ready for school. Mr
Tarboy kept an old car parked by the bank
and when it was raining he drove them to
school, but when it was fine they walked.

This morning it was raining so he took them.
Later, the sun came out, so they walked
home. The lane was full of puddles which
they tried to jump, but mostly missed,
splashing happily as they went.

Close to home, Tom found an old
microwave oven dumped in the hedge.
He thought his mother might like it.

'It won't work, daftie!' Emily said.
'That's why the travellers threw it out.'

She walked on to the
end of the hedge and saw
the old pony tethered to
a rusty anchor with
a long piece of rope.
The pony looked at her
and whinnied.

'Paddy, you poor
thing. They've left you
behind!' she cried.

Emily went up to
him and gave him
the last bit of her
Kit Kat bar from her
pocket. Paddy
nuzzled at her
pockets for more,
and licked her fingers.
His coat was all
matted and muddy
and in spite of its
thickness, you could
see his ribs.

Even Tom, who wasn't soppy about animals like Emily, thought that leaving the pony behind was a rotten thing to do. They went and told their mother and she came out on to the bank to have a look.

'Well, someone's got to look after him,' she said. 'Why don't you go and tell Mr Barber? Perhaps he can put Paddy in his barn.'

Mr Barber was the farmer who lived further along the bank. Tom and Emily ran and told him but he didn't want to know about Paddy and said they should tell the police. Emily burst into tears, and Mrs Barber told her husband he was heartless. She told him to give Emily a bale of hay so that at least the pony wouldn't starve. So Mr Barber drove the children back in his Land Rover with a bale of hay which he put in Mr Tarboy's bits and pieces shed.

'Feed him a bit at a time. It'll only get

trampled otherwise. And give him a bucket of water with it.'

Mrs Tarboy said Mr Barber's bark was worse than his bite and she helped Emily give Paddy a bundle of the hay and a bucket of water. Emily put her arms round Paddy's scrawny neck and said, 'Don't worry. I'm going to look after you. I shall pretend you're mine.'

Paddy cheered up quite a lot.

Chapter Two

EMILY, AND EVEN Tom, liked the idea of having their own pony, and Mr and Mrs Tarboy let them feed and water the pony for the next few days.

'It's not right though,' Mrs Tarboy said. 'He needs proper shelter, an old pony like that.'

They asked around, but no one in the village wanted to take on a broken-down old pony in the middle of winter. Paddy's patch of grass grew wetter and muddier, even though the children kept moving the tether.

'Perhaps we should ask Mr Barber again,'
Mrs Tarboy said anxiously.

That night it rained very hard, with lumps of
hail that pinged on the deck. Stormy weather
was forecast, so Mr Tarboy went out to look
at his mooring warps. He knew the tide
would come in before dawn and the houseboat would float high and pull and tug at her
ropes in the wind. Now the tide was out and
the boat rested on the mud. Paddy stood on
the grass beside the boat with his tail to the
wind and his head down, a picture of misery.
Mr Tarboy stood looking at him sadly.

He said to his wife, 'If he'll come up the
gangplank, he can stand in my bits and pieces
shed tonight, out of the wind, with his bale
of hay.'

Emily heard this and shouted, 'Yes! Yes!
Please! Do bring him in!'

'Good idea,' Mrs Tarboy said. 'I wouldn't
want to be treated like that when I'm old.'

'We'll try it,' said Mr Tarboy.

Tom and Emily danced with excitement.

They wanted to rush outside and help, but
Mrs Tarboy made them watch out of the
window. They saw their father go out into
the storm, then appear in a few minutes on
top of the bank, holding Paddy by his rope.
The gangplank stretched down before them,
wide and stout. Mr Tarboy walked on to it
and encouraged Paddy to follow.
The pony stood there in the rain, his
mane and tail blowing out in the
wind, hesitating. Then he put
one small hoof on the plank.
Very nervously he took
a step forward.

'He's coming! He's
coming!' Emily shouted.

'He knows where
he's well off,' Mrs
Tarboy said.

Mr Tarboy went
ahead, encouraging
him, holding him
on his tether rope,

and cautiously Paddy followed him down
the plank.

In a moment he was on the deck, looking
round curiously. Tom and Emily cheered.

They quickly bundled
themselves into their
outdoor clothes and
rushed outside to help
their father clear a
corner in the shed.
Tucked behind the big
wheel-house, the shed
was dry and out of the
wind, and there was a

sack of wood shavings that Mr Tarboy laid
down for a bed. Paddy was happy in his
new stable with the bundle
of hay to eat. The rain
and hail dinned on the
roof but he was dry
and warm. Emily
hugged him and
Mrs Tarboy brought
him some carrots
from the galley.

'I don't know that we
can make a habit of

this,' she said. But she laughed all the same, and they all went below out of the storm.

The wind grew stronger as the night progressed. The tide started to rise. Tom and Emily went to bed, but their father stayed up, worrying about his mooring ropes.

'Well, there's nothing more you can do, dear. You might as well come to bed,' Mrs Tarboy said.

'I'd rather stay here until the storm quietens down,' Mr Tarboy replied.

'I don't know why you worry about your old boat so much,' Mrs Tarboy mumbled as she went off to bed.

So Mr Tarboy stayed up and dozed in his armchair in front of the fire, and the rest of the family slept.

In his cosy shed, Paddy lay down on his bed of wood shavings and dreamt of his early days when he was young. Then he had lived in a beautiful stable and there was a family to love him and ride him over the downs. What a long time ago! Nobody had loved him for a long time.

After a while his new stable started to move up and down in a rather curious way and he wondered what was happening. He got up and looked out. He saw a wild expanse of water with white waves breaking, very close, which he thought very strange. The stable seemed to be moving along, but he couldn't quite see why. He thought perhaps it was like a horse box, driving

through the countryside. However he still had
a roof over his head and the rain and hail
weren't coming in, so why should he worry?
It was a lot better than that muddy field.

Mr Tarboy had dozed for quite a while.
He woke with a start.

Immediately he knew something was wrong.

There was no jerking of the mooring ropes
or creaking of timbers as there usually was at
a rough high tide. And the boat
seemed to be moving.

'We're adrift!' he
muttered, and he
rushed up
on deck.

It was quite true. There was no sign of the
gangplank or the land. All he could see were
heaving waves with foaming white tops, lit
by the light of a full moon coming and going
through the clouds. The boat was at sea,
plunging through the big waves as if back in
her old life, carrying a cargo down the coast.
But now she was old and unfit for rough seas.
Then Mr Tarboy remembered they had
a pony on board!

He hurried up to the wheel-house and
looked round the back of it into his shed.
The pony stood foursquare, hooves firmly
planted, eating his hay. He looked at
Mr Tarboy and gave a little whinny.

'Hello, old fellow,' said Mr Tarboy.
'We're in a fine pickle. Don't you go taking
off now, else you'll have a long swim for it.'

Mr Tarboy knew he had to go and look for
his anchor to throw overboard and stop the
boat going farther
out to sea. But the
anchor hadn't been
used for a long
time and the chain
wasn't attached.
He fetched a lamp
and started looking
for the chain.
Mrs Tarboy heard
him and got up to
see what was
going on. When
she looked out,
she nearly died of
fright. But her
husband calmed
her down and told
her to help him pull
out the chain.

By this time it had stopped raining and Paddy had finished his hay. He put his head round the side of his shed and decided to explore this strange new place. He walked out along the deck and stood in the bows, holding his head up to the wind. His mane and tail blew out and his eyes shone in the darkness. He felt he had new life in his old bones. It was a long time since anything exciting had happened to him. The moon came and went between the whistling clouds, and the storm crackled in his ears. 'What a lucky pony I am!' he thought, lifting his nose to the wind.

Meanwhile, Mrs Tarboy was helping her husband heave the heavy anchor up through the hatch.

'Whatever will happen to us?' she cried. 'I always said we should live in a proper house!'

'When the anchor goes down, we'll stop where we are. And in the morning when the tide turns, we'll pull the anchor up and go back up the river,' Mr Tarboy said.

They climbed out of the hatch and found Paddy standing there looking out to sea. He didn't seem to be at all afraid. Mrs Tarboy was amazed. She had forgotten all about Paddy.

But Mr Tarboy said, 'Don't bother with him now. Help me get this anchor overboard.'

He attached the big heavy chain and together they lifted the anchor and dropped it overboard. The chain ran out with a great rattle as the anchor dropped to the bottom. Then the anchor dug in and the boat stopped. The tide and the waves raced past but the boat stayed in place, anchored to the bottom of the sea.

'Thank goodness for that,' said Mrs Tarboy.

She went back to bed, but Mr Tarboy stayed up all night to keep watch. The old boat tossed on the waves and the anchor chain danced and groaned all night, tugging at the anchor, but it held the boat and stopped it from drifting further out to sea. Paddy went back to his shed out of the wind and fell asleep on his nice wood shavings bed.

Chapter Three

WHEN TOM AND Emily woke up in the morning and looked out of their porthole there was no land to be seen! Blue sea stretched to the horizon, and huge white clouds floated serenely across the sky. Their father was down in the engine room trying to get the engine to go, and their mother was cooking breakfast in the galley. Tom and Emily raced on deck to look out.

'No school today!' Tom shouted. 'School is miles away!'

'How lucky we brought Paddy on board,'
Emily said, 'or there wouldn't be anyone to
give him his hay.'

She fed him and filled his water bucket.
'Aren't you lucky? Not many ponies go
sailing,' she told him.

They went down below for their breakfast, and soon they heard the chug-chug of the engine as their father coaxed it into life.

'Thank goodness, we shall be able to motor back to our mooring,' said Mrs Tarboy. 'All's well that ends well.'

'We've got to get the anchor up first,'
Mr Tarboy said. 'It's going to be hard work.
All hands on deck!'

They all had to go and help pull,
even Emily.

But pull as they might, they could only get
in a few metres of chain. The water was deep
and the anchor a long way down.

'One! Two! Three! Heave!' shouted
Mr Tarboy.

'Heave!' shouted Tom and Emily.

They all heaved, but nothing happened.

They tried again. And again. And again.
But each time they only pulled in a few feet
of chain. Mr Tarboy was very worried.

'Looks like we're stuck here!'

'We've got no bread and only half a pint
of milk,' said Mrs Tarboy. 'Whatever shall
we do?'

Even Tom and Emily thought of school, but
where was the land? All round them was
sparkling sea, and their boat – although it was
their house – seemed very small, bobbing
gently up and down on the waves.

Then Tom had a great idea.

'Paddy!' he shouted. 'He can pull! That's what ponies are for!'

'I believe he did pull a cart for the travellers,' Mr Tarboy said. 'I used to see him in the summer.'

'Good idea, Tom. You go and fetch the pony and I'll find a stout bit of rope.'

He went below to the rope locker and Tom and Emily put Paddy's halter on and led him up the deck.

'You've got to do some work, Paddy,'
Tom said.

'Earn your keep,' said Mrs Tarboy.

Mr Tarboy brought the big rope up from
below and attached it to Paddy. He tied the
other end to the anchor chain.

'You've got to pull, old fellow, like a plough
horse. You remember plough horses? I reckon
you're old enough!'

Mr Tarboy laughed and turned Paddy round
so that he was facing the other way, and his
rope was taut to the anchor chain.

'Now, all together – and Paddy too –'

'Heave!' shouted Tom.

'Heave!' shouted Emily.

Paddy soon got the idea. He dug his hooves
into the deck and heaved with all 'his
strength. He had often pulled heavy loads for
the travellers and he knew how to put his
head down and throw his weight into the
collar. The rope bit into his chest but he did
not flinch.

'Heave!' shouted Mr Tarboy.

And there was a clank clank from the bows
as the great chain began to grind in.

'Heave!' shouted Tom.

'Heave!' shouted Emily.

Mrs Tarboy's arms bulged as she pulled.

Mr Tarboy groaned and the sweat flew
from his brow.

Paddy put down his head and pretended
he was a plough horse, and heaved with
all his might.

Slowly, steadily, link after link the big chain
clanked onto the boat until the anchor was in.

Chapter Four

AT LAST PADDY could rest. The anchor hung
on the bows, dripping with weed and mud.
Paddy stood dripping with sweat. Mrs Tarboy
sat down in a heap on the deck, panting for
breath and Mr Tarboy wiped his brow and
said, 'My word, that was a good effort, eh?'

Mr Tarboy and Emily lifted the heavy rope
off Paddy's chest and, while Tom put it neatly
away, Emily rubbed Paddy's sore places
and fetched him some sugar lumps from
the galley.

'You're a good, brave pony and you've
saved us!' she said.

'Saved our bacon!' said Mr Tarboy.

'Worth his weight in gold!' said Mrs Tarboy.

'Gold Medal Paddy,' said Tom.

Mr Tarboy went to the wheel-house and put
the engine into gear and the old houseboat
chugged back in from the sea towards her
mooring place.

Mrs Tarboy made some coffee and got
out the biscuits and Tom and Emily sat
in the bows with Paddy standing
between them.

The sun, now warm and soft,
dried Paddy's sweaty coat and
lifted his mane gently off his
neck to blow in the breeze.
Paddy could smell shore
smells of warm grass and
damp earth. The bad
winter was nearly over
and he had found some
good friends.

Tom and Emily shared their biscuits with him.

'You're our pony now, Paddy,' Emily said, 'and we shall look after you.'

'That we will,' said Mrs Tarboy, coming up with a sugar lump. 'That pony saved our lives. He's got a home with us for as long as he needs it.'

And the Tarboys found Paddy a lovely grassy field in the village by the school, with a cow and a goat for company. Tom and Emily visited him every day, and when the weather was bad they brought him back to the bits and pieces shed on board. And the people in the village called him Paddy the sailor, the pony that went to sea.

Have you enjoyed this Yellow Banana? There are plenty more to read. Why not try one of these exciting new stories:

A Funny sort of Dog *by Elizabeth Laird*
There's something not quite right about Simon's new puppy, Tip. It's very big with long claws, and it roars. Then one day it climbs a tree and Simon has to face the truth . . . perhaps Tip isn't a dog at all!

Ghostly Guests *by Penelope Lively*
When the Brown family move to a new house, Marion and Simon discover there are three ghosts already living there! The ghosts make their lives unbearable – how can the children get rid of them?

Carole's Camel *by Michael Hardcastle*
Carole is left a rather unusual present – a camel called Umberto. It's great to ride him to school and everyone loves him, even if he is rather smelly. But looking after a real camel can cause a lot of problems. Perhaps she should find him a more suitable home . . .

Ollie and the Trainers *by Rachel Anderson*
Ollie has two problems: he has no trainers and he can't read. Dad agrees to buy him some trainers but they turn out to be no ordinary pair. They are Secret Readers and can talk! Can Leftfoot Peter and Rightfoot Paul help Ollie to read?

Bella's Den *by Berlie Doherty*
Moving to the country, my only friend is Bella. One day she shows me her secret – a den. We go there one night and see some foxes, and in my excitement I blurt out what I've seen and a farmer overhears. He says foxes kill lambs and later he sets off to hunt them down. I've got to stop him . . .